THE SNAIL'S SPELL

by Joanne Ryder

Pictures by Lynne Cherry

PUFFIN BOOKS

PUFFIN BOOKS
A Division of Penguin Books USA Inc.
375 Hudson Street, New York, New York 10014
Penguin Books Ltd, 27 Wrights Lane, London W8 5TZ England
Penguin Books Australia Ltd, Ringwood, Victoria, Australia
Penguin Books Canada Ltd, 10 Alcorn Avenue, Toronto, Ontario, Canada M4V 3B2
Penguin Books (N.Z.) Ltd, 182–190 Wairau Road, Auckland 10, New Zealand

Penguin Books Ltd, Registered Offices: Harmondsworth, Middlesex, England

First published in the United States of America by Frederick Warne & Co., Inc., 1982
Published in Puffin Books 1988
20 19 18 17 16 15 14 13 12
Text copyright © Joanne Ryder, 1982
Illustrations copyright © Lynne Cherry, 1982

Library of Congress Cataloging-in-Publication Data
Ryder, Joanne.
The snail's spell/by Joanne Ryder; pictures by Lynne Cherry.
p. cm.
Summary: The reader imagines how it feels to be a snail.
ISBN 0-14-050891-0
1. Snails—Juvenile fiction. [1. Snails—Fiction] I. Cherry, Lynne, ill. II. Title.
PZ10.3.R954Sn 1988
[E]—dc19   87-32869

Color separations by Imago Ltd., Hong Kong
Printed in the United States of America
Set in Goudy Oldstyle

To my cousins,
Brett
Douglas
Eric
Erin
James
Jeffrey
Kelly
Matthew
Meghan
Melanie
Shaun

J.R.

To Bessie Cogan,
my wonderful
grandmother.

L.C.

Imagine
you are soft
and have no bones
inside you.
Imagine
you are grey,
the color of smoke.

You are shrinking

smaller
and
smaller
and
smaller.

You are two inches long,
lying on the brown ground
all soft and grey.
Imagine you have no arms
and legs now.
Imagine you
cannot walk or run.

Instead you glide
and make your own
smooth sticky path
to ride on.
It is easy
to move this way
and it feels
cool and good.

BROCCOLI

You have a head
and a mouth
with rows of tiny teeth—
but your teeth are on your tongue!
You eat
by sticking out your tongue
and scraping
tiny bits of lettuce
into your tiny mouth.

BROCCOLI

As you glide slowly
on the damp brown ground,
you touch everything
with two short feelers.

On the top of your head
you have two long feelers.
You can stretch and stretch
these feelers
till they look like
long, long horns.

Your small black eyes
rest at the tips of these feelers.
One eye sees the brightness above.
The other feeler
curls around a lettuce leaf.
Now you can see the darkness there.

But your feeler
touches something in the dark,
something wriggling,
someone alive!
Fast as you can
you pull your feeler back.
You tuck your eye
inside your feeler
and hide it from danger.
Your eye glides
down and down
into your head.

When you feel safe,
your eye glides
up and up
to see your world again.
You are soft and small and slow
gliding up and down
and upside down.

On your back
lies a light, curled shell.
It is part of you
and it grows
as you grow.

Sanislo Elementary

Whenever you want to rest,
you have a place to go.
First you tuck your feelers
inside your head.
Then you draw your head
and soft, grey body
inside your shell
and sleep.